# Eliza
# the Hypnotizer

## AND OTHER ELIZA AND FRANCIE STORIES

*by Michele Granger*

*Illustrated by*
*Gioia Fiammenghi*

A
**LITTLE APPLE**
PAPERBACK

## SCHOLASTIC INC.

New York  Toronto  London  Auckland  Sydney

With love for Lindsay,
who knows what it's like
to be the little sister.
— M.G.

No part of this publication may be reproduced in whole or in part, or stored in a retrieval system, or transmitted in any form or by any means, electronic, mechanical, photocopying, recording, or otherwise, without written permission of the publisher. For information regarding permission, write to Scholastic Inc., 730 Broadway, New York, NY 10003.

ISBN 0-590-45506-0

12  11  10  9  8  7  6  5  4  3  2  1        3  4  5  6  7  8/9

Printed in the U.S.A.                              28

First Scholastic printing, February 1993

# Contents

# 1.
# Eliza the Hypnotizer

Eliza swung Zazu's catnip mouse by its tail. Back and forth. Back and forth. Zazu swiped at it. Then she just watched.

"Look, Francie," Eliza said to her sister. "I'm hypnotizing the cat."

"Sure you are," said Francie.

Eliza's arm got tired of swinging. She dropped the mouse at Zazu's feet. Zazu ignored it.

"Bring your mouse to Francie, Zazu," said Eliza.

Zazu did.

"Did you see that?" Eliza asked. "Zazu is hypnotized!"

"You've completely lost your mind," Francie told her.

Eliza whispered in Zazu's ear. "Go get Francie's lilac hair ribbon and bring it down here."

Zazu yawned. Then she went.

"She's going!" Eliza ran after her.

Francie kept reading.

Thrip. Thrip. Thrip. Zazu came back down the stairs. Eliza followed her. Zazu carried Francie's ribbon in her mouth.

"I can't believe it!" said Eliza. "She did it!"

"And I can't believe that you're touching my ribbon," said Francie.

Eliza handed the ribbon over.

"I heard you on the stairs, Eliza," said Francie.

"It was Zazu," said Eliza. "She carried the ribbon down in her mouth."

"There are no teethmarks on this ribbon, Eliza."

"I told Zazu to be gentle with it," said Eliza. "And she does whatever I tell her. She's hypnotized."

"Right," said Francie. "Then why don't you have her clean up your room? Mom wants it done before she gets back."

"Okay. I will," Eliza said. "I mean, Zazu will. C'mon, Zazu."

Zazu followed Eliza up the stairs. Zazu dusted the bookcase while Eliza made the bed.

"Francie," Eliza called down. "She's doing it. Zazu's cleaning my room."

"Of course," said Francie. "And the goldfish is singing down here."

"Now she's sweeping the floor!" Eliza shouted. "Come see!"

"Give me a break, Eliza. I'm on my last chapter."

"She's straightening my dresser drawers!" said Eliza. "I can't believe you're missing this!"

"Believe it," said Francie.

"She's finished," Eliza announced. "Do you want Zazu to clean your room?"

"Sure," said Francie. "Clean my room, Zazu."

Zazu licked her paw.

"She'll only do it if *I* tell her," Eliza said.

"Then tell her. And let me read in peace."

"Zazu," said Eliza. "Clean Francie's room now.

"She's dusting your china horses, Francie. Zazu's really doing it."

"Break one of my horses and I'll really do it to you, Eliza."

"I'm not touching them," Eliza told her. "Zazu's dusting and she's being very careful."

"Sure she is," said Francie.

"Finished!" Eliza sang out. "Do you want Zazu to tidy up your closet, Francie?"

"Stay out of my closet, Eliza. I've got three pages left. Will you please shut up?"

"Oh, I won't go in," said Eliza. "Zazu will do it. And Mom doesn't want you to say 'shut up,' Francie."

"She probably doesn't want you hypnotizing the cat, either," Francie said.

"You think I'm kidding," said Eliza. "But Zazu's really hypnotized."

"I know you're kidding," said Francie. "Now, *fermez la bouche.*"

"What?"

"That's French for 'shut up.' And I mean it. I'm on my last page."

"Done!" Eliza shouted. "Your room looks beautiful. Come, look."

"Done!" Francie closed her book. "Zazu, here I come!"

Francie ran up the stairs.

"Eliza, my room looks terrific," she

said. "I mean it. It really does."

"Tell Zazu," said Eliza. "She did most of the work."

"Zazu," said Francie, "my room looks terrific."

"Zazu's a wonderful cat," said Eliza.

"And you're a wonderful little sister," said Francie. "Thanks for cleaning my room, Eliza."

"You still don't believe me."

"I believe you," said Francie. "I believe that you are totally crazy."

"I hypnotized our cat," said Eliza.

"Right," said Francie. "Want to play a game of Fish till Mom gets home?"

"Sure," said Eliza. "Can Zazu play, too?"

"Oh, why not?" said Francie. "She doesn't cheat, does she?"

"Only if I tell her to," said Eliza.

# 2.
# Knock-Knock

"**K**nock-knock," said Eliza.

"Oh, no," said Francie. "Not another one of your knock-knock jokes."

"C'mon," said Eliza. "Just *one* more?"

"*One* more," said Francie. "And that's it. I'm trying to write a letter."

"I promise. This is the *last* one," said Eliza. "Ready, Francie?"

Francie sighed. "Ready."

"You're going to love this one," said Eliza. "It's funny."

Francie slammed down her pen. "Will you just *tell* it?"

"Okay." Eliza cleared her throat. "Knock-knock."

"Who's there?"

"Eyes."

Francie sounded bored. "Eyes who?"

Eliza grinned. "Eyes got another knock-knock joke for you."

"No way," Francie told her. "You promised."

"But it's part of the same joke," Eliza said.

"You're a pain, Eliza, you know it?" said Francie. "A real pain."

"Please? Please? Please?" Eliza begged. "Can I just finish it?"

"When it's done, will you go away and let me write my letter?" Francie asked.

"Yes," Eliza said. "If you let me finish, I'll leave you alone."

"Well . . ." Francie said. "Okay."

"Great," said Eliza. "Knock-knock."

"Who's there?" Francie asked as if she didn't care a bit.

"Nose."

Francie yawned. "Nose who?"

Eliza giggled. "I nose another knock-knock joke."

"Forget it," said Francie. "You tricked me, Eliza."

"And you said that I could finish, Francie."

Francie picked up her pen and began to write.

Eliza stamped her foot. "You *promised*."

Francie kept writing.

"It's not funny if I don't do the whole joke," Eliza said.

"It's not funny, period," said Francie.

"But the *best* part is at the end," Eliza said.

"When *is* the end?" Francie asked.

"We're almost there," said Eliza.

"And when the joke is finished, you'll go away, right?"

"Right," Eliza said. "Ready?"

Francie nodded.

"Knock-knock."

"Who's there?"

"Ears."

"Ears who?"

Eliza began to laugh. "Ears another knock-knock joke."

Francie put her head in her hands. "Why do I let you do this to me?"

"Almost done! Almost done!" Eliza cried. "C'mon, Francie, knock-knock."

Francie's voice came through her fingers. "Who's there?"

"Chin."

"Chin who?"

"Chin up," said Eliza. "I'm not going to tell any more knock-knock jokes."

Francie lifted her head. "Hooray!" she said. "Now, get out of here."

"I'm going," Eliza told her.

But in a minute, she was back. She knocked twice on Francie's door. Knock-knock.

"Go away!" Francie said.

"Aren't you going to ask who it is?" said Eliza.

"I *know* who it is."

Eliza knocked twice again. Knock-knock.

*"Eliza!"*

"Please, say it?" Eliza begged.

She knocked twice again. Knock-knock.

"Oh, for goodness' sake!" Francie yelled. "Who's there?"

"Tank," Eliza answered.

"Tank who?"

"Tank who for letting me tell my knock-knock jokes, Francie."

"You're welcome," said Francie. "Now, go!"

"Okay." Eliza started down the hall.

Francie opened her door. "Hey, Eliza," she called.

"What?"

"That one was pretty funny," Francie said.

"Tank who," said Eliza. "Tank who very much."

# 3.
# Out to Lunch

"Ick. I can't eat it," Eliza said.

Francie took a long breath and let it out. "It's what you ordered."

"But they gave me coleslaw," Eliza whined.

"You *like* coleslaw, Eliza."

"Yes, but . . ."

"But *what?*"

"It's touching my hamburger," said Eliza.

Francie looked. "There's not one bit of coleslaw touching your hamburger."

"But that white stuff . . ."

"It's just dressing," Francie told her.

"It's heading for my hamburger," Eliza said.

"Well, move it over."

"Too late! See? It's touching." Eliza stared miserably at her plate. "Now I have nothing to eat."

"If we get you something else, we won't have any money left for dessert," said Francie.

"You don't care," Eliza said. "Your lunch is great. Nothing's touching anything."

Francie sighed. "I told Mom this would never work."

"What?"

"Taking *you* out for lunch. You're so picky, Eliza."

"I like this restaurant," said Eliza. "I just don't like my food."

"So, what do you want — *my* lunch?" asked Francie.

"Well . . ." said Eliza. "I like that nothing's touching."

"Take it." Francie traded her plate for Eliza's. "Have my hot dog. I'll eat your hamburger. I'm not picky like you."

"Thanks, Francie. You're the best big sister in the world."

"Just eat your lunch. Okay, Eliza? Everyone's looking at us."

"They are not," said Eliza.

"Eat!"

"You're the one who's yelling, Francie."

Eliza looked at her hot dog. But she didn't pick it up.

"Eliza," said Francie. "Why aren't you eating your hot dog?"

"I will," said Eliza.

"When?"

"When I'm ready."

Francie rolled her eyes. "Go ahead. Tell me what's wrong with it."

"These aren't the kind of buns Mom uses," said Eliza.

"If you want the kind that Mom uses, you should stay home and eat," said Francie.

"This one smells funny," Eliza told her.

"Do not smell your food like that, Eliza. It's disgusting!"

"No one saw," said Eliza.

"Of course they did," said Francie. "Someone always sees when you do something dumb."

Francie pulled Eliza's hot dog out of its bun and set it on her plate.

"Do you want me to cut it up for you?"

"No."

"You can't pick it up in your hand to eat it," Francie said. "Not in a restaurant."

"I know," said Eliza.

"So?"

Eliza rolled the hot dog back and forth with one finger.

"They cooked it too much," she said.

"I give up," said Francie. "Just eat the chips, and we'll get dessert."

"What kind of a lunch is that?" said Eliza.

"The kind you're having," said Francie. "Now, please, eat something. Eat anything. Just eat."

Eliza picked up a chip. She took one bite. Then, she put it down.

"Well?" said Francie.

"Pickle juice," Eliza said. "It got in the chips."

Francie closed her eyes.

The waitress came up to their table.

"Do you girls want dessert?" she asked.

"Yes!" Francie told her. "We do."

"The apple pie is very good," the waitress said. "How about pie á la mode?"

"What's that?" asked Eliza.

"It's a piece of pie with vanilla ice cream on top," the waitress said.

"Oh, *I'll* have that," said Eliza.

"You *will?*" said Francie. "But, Eliza, it's touching."

"Yes," said Eliza. "I'll have it in two dishes. One for the pie, and one for the ice cream."

"And what will *you* have?" the waitress asked Francie.

"Nothing," said Francie. "I'm not so hungry anymore."

# 4.
# The Scary Sound

"Francie," Eliza whispered. "Did you hear that?"

Francie was almost asleep. "Go back to bed," she said.

"But I *heard* something."

Francie put her pillow over her head.

"I'm scared," Eliza said. "Can I sleep with you?"

Francie's voice was hard to hear. "No."

"I won't take up much room," Eliza told her. "I'm little."

Francie came out from under her pillow. "And I'm big. I need the whole bed."

Eliza wouldn't leave. "Please? Just this once?"

"That's what you said last time," Francie reminded her.

"But this time, I *mean* it."

"You said *that* last time, too," Francie said. "Take Zazu to bed with you."

"She's scared, too," Eliza said. "Aren't you, Zazu?"

Zazu curled her tail around her. She lay down on Francie's rug and closed her eyes.

"She looks simply terrified," said Francie.

"She's just pretending not to be," said Eliza.

"Good idea," said Francie. "Why don't you pretend not to be, too?"

"I can't."

"Why not?"

"Because I'm really, *really* scared. Can I please come in?"

"No."

"I won't move," Eliza promised. "You won't even know I'm there."

"Yes, I will."

"How?"

"I'll hear you breathing."

"I won't breathe, then," said Eliza.

"Don't be ridiculous," said Francie. "You *have* to breathe."

"I'll breathe very, *very* quietly," Eliza said.

"And you'll drool on my pillow," Francie said.

"I don't drool anymore," said Eliza.

"You did *last* time."

"I was a little kid then."

"It was three nights ago, Eliza."

"Oh." Eliza didn't leave. She stood next to Francie's bed. She practiced breathing quietly.

"You'll tear up my legs with your toe-nails," Francie said. "You have claws for toenails."

"I have my feet pajamas on. See?" Eliza held up one foot.

"Okay," Francie said. "Here's the deal. You lie perfectly still on *your* side of the bed. You breathe very, *very* quietly. You don't drool and you don't say *one* word."

"It's a deal." Eliza stuck out her hand. "Want to shake on it?"

Francie moved over. "Just get in."

"Thanks, Francie." Eliza climbed into bed and pulled up the covers.

Francie yanked the blankets back. "Don't hog the covers, either," she said. "I forgot to say that."

"I won't," Eliza promised.

Francie rolled over and faced the wall.

"Francie . . ." Eliza began.

"Not *one* word!"

"I was wondering . . ."

"*What*, Eliza?"

"Will you trade places with me? I don't like to be on the outside."

"Why not?"

"Something could get me out here."

"And you want it to get me first, is that it?" Francie asked.

"You're bigger," Eliza said.

"That's right," said Francie. "I'm bigger and I need my whole bed. I never should have let you in."

"Francie . . ."

"M-m-m-m . . ." Francie pretended to be asleep.

"Ple-e-e-ase?"

"All right! All right! Move, so I can get out."

Eliza did. Then she took Francie's place on the inside, and Francie took Eliza's place on the outside.

"That's better," Eliza said. "Thanks, Francie."

"Sh-h-h-h!"

Eliza snuggled down into Francie's bed.

She made herself as small as she could. She kept her feet away from Francie's. She breathed very, *very* quietly. She didn't say one word.

Then, Francie heard something. A scary sound.

"Did you hear that, Eliza?" she whispered.

Eliza didn't answer. She was fast asleep.

Francie moved closer to her sister. She could hear Eliza breathing. She was drooling on Francie's pillow, too. And Francie was so glad to have her there.

# 5.
# The Last Candy Bar

"**Y**ou're lying, Eliza," Francie said.

"Am not."

"I know you still have some Halloween candy left."

"I ate it already," Eliza told her.

"You did not."

"So?"

"So, mine's all gone," Francie said. "It's been gone for days. I'm desperate for chocolate, Eliza. Please?"

"No."

"Just a half?" Francie begged.

"It's my *last* candy bar," Eliza said.

"A teeny, tiny piece?"

"Why should I give you my last candy bar just because you're a big pig and ate all yours?" Eliza asked.

"I am not a pig," said Francie. "But I *am* bigger. I need more chocolate than you."

"What'll you give me?" Eliza wanted to know.

"*Give* you?"

"Yes," said Eliza. "If I give you some of my candy bar, what'll you give me back?"

Francie rested her chin in her hand. "H-m-m-m . . ."

"Well?"

"I'm thinking," Francie told her.

"How about one of your china horses?" Eliza suggested.

"For half a candy bar? Are you crazy?"

"It's my last one," Eliza said. "My very last Halloween candy bar."

"No!"

"Just a small one?" Eliza said. "A colt?"

"I said 'no'! Think of something else," Francie said.

Eliza thought for a minute. Then, she shook her head. "I can't."

"Oh, c'mon, Eliza. There must be something."

"A china horse is all I want."

"Well," said Francie. "You can't have one."

"Then, I guess you can't have any of my candy bar," said Eliza.

Francie held her stomach. "I'm starving, Eliza. It's mean not to give someone food when they're hungry."

"Just one little horse," said Eliza. "I'd even take an ugly one."

"I don't have any ugly horses," Francie said. "They're all beautiful."

"What about the skinny little yellow one?" asked Eliza.

"It's tan and it's not skinny and you can't have it."

"Okay." Eliza put her candy bar into her desk drawer and shut it.

"Aren't you hungry, Eliza?"

Eliza thought about it. "M-m-m-m. A little."

"Wouldn't you love some of that yummy candy bar right now?" Francie asked.

"I told you what I want," Eliza said.

"But it's too much," said Francie. "A china horse for half a candy bar is not a fair trade."

"Can I play with your horses, then?" Eliza asked.

"You'll break them," Francie said. "They're not for little kids."

"I'm *not* a little kid," said Eliza.

"Yes, you are."

"Well," said Eliza. "I'm a little kid with a candy bar that you want, so you'd better be nice to me."

Francie flopped on Eliza's bed. "Okay."

"Okay, what?" Eliza asked.

"Okay. You can play with my horses," said Francie. "But I have to play, too."

"Really, Francie?" Eliza could never get Francie to play with her.

"I have to make sure you don't break any," Francie said.

"I won't. You'll see." Eliza opened her desk drawer and took out the candy bar.

Francie sat up. "Go ahead. Open it."

"Wait a minute," said Eliza. "Are you going to say, 'I don't want to play anymore' after just a little while?"

"No," said Francie. "I promise. Now, give me the candy."

Eliza put the candy bar down on her desk. "I think I'll save it."

Francie jumped up. "Save it for *when?*"

"For when we're done playing," Eliza said. "I'll give you some then. I promise."

"But I'm hungry *now*," Francie said.

"Then let's hurry up and play," said Eliza.

And they did.

When they were finished playing, Eliza gave Francie the bigger piece of her candy bar. "You're right, Francie," she said. "You're bigger. You do need more chocolate."

# 6.
# The Chicken Pox Cake

"**I** can't believe you have chicken pox, Eliza," Francie said from the doorway.

Eliza lay back on her pillow. "Me, either."

"Now I'll probably get them!"

"Maybe you won't."

"I've made it all the way to sixth grade without getting chicken pox," Francie said.

"A lot of kids in my class have them," Eliza said.

"But you're a little kid, Eliza. It's okay for little kids to get them."

"It doesn't feel okay," Eliza told her. "They itch."

"It would be so embarrassing if I got them," said Francie.

"They itch a *lot*," Eliza said.

"All I need are more zits on my face," said Francie. "Look at you. You look like a pizza."

"You're not being very nice to me, Francie."

"Nice!" said Francie. "How can I be nice when I'm so upset?"

"Not nice at *all*."

Francie held out her arms. "You don't see any on me, do you?"

"No." Then Eliza looked at her own arms. "But I bet I've got a million of them."

Francie leaned into Eliza's room to get a better look. "At *least* a million," she said. "You look awful."

"I *feel* awful," Eliza told her. "I'm itchy and hot and I feel awful."

"You're hot?" Francie asked. "I'm cold. Do you think that means I've got a chill? Do you think that means I'm getting chicken pox?"

"I think it means you should put on a sweater," said Eliza. "And then go away and leave me alone. You don't even care that I'm sick."

"Oh, Eliza," said Francie. "You're right. I'm only thinking about me, and you're the one who has chicken pox."

"I do," Eliza agreed. "I have them all over me."

"Why don't you take a nice oatmeal bath?" Francie suggested. "I'll get it ready for you."

"No," said Eliza. "I'm too tired."

"Why don't you take a nap, then?" Francie asked.

And for once, that seemed like a very good idea.

Eliza pulled the covers up to her chin and went to sleep.

When she opened her eyes again, Francie was back in the doorway.

"Finally!" Francie said. "I thought you'd never wake up."

"Do you have chicken pox yet?" Eliza asked.

"No," said Francie. "I made you something."

"What?"

"It's to cheer you up." Francie ran off and came back with a cake on a plate. It had one lighted candle stuck in it.

"You didn't make that," Eliza said. "Mom did."

"Mom made just a plain old cake," Francie said. "But *I* made it into a Chicken Pox Cake."

"A Chicken Pox Cake?"

"Pull the covers over your head while I bring it to you," Francie said. "I don't want your chicken pox germs on me."

Eliza pulled the covers over her head.

Francie took the cake and set it on the table by Eliza's bed. Then she ran back to the doorway.

"Okay. You can come out!" she said. Then, from the doorway, she sang:

"Happy chicken pox to you.

Happy chicken pox to you.

You look like a pizza

Hope I don't get them, too!"

Eliza looked. "It *is* a Chicken Pox Cake," she said.

"I *told* you. Now, quick, blow out the candle."

Eliza closed her eyes. She made a wish, just like on her birthday. Then she blew out the candle.

"Know what I wished?" she asked.

"Don't tell," said Francie. "Don't tell."

"I wished *you* wouldn't get chicken pox," said Eliza.

"You dope," said Francie. "If you tell, your wish doesn't come true."

"I know," said Eliza. "But don't worry, Francie. When you get them, I'll make you a Chicken Pox Cake, too."

# How to Make a
# Chicken Pox Cake

## What You Need

1. One round cake, any flavor.
   (Eliza's mom made devil's food, Eliza and
   Francie's favorite.)

2. Frosting to cover the cake's top and sides, in
   a color like the chicken pox person's skin.
   (Francie used vanilla.)

3. A small amount of frosting the color of the
   chicken pox person's hair.
   (Francie used chocolate.)

**4.** Two candies for eyes.
(Francie used purple gumdrops because they don't make blue ones. If your chicken pox person's eyes are green, you're lucky because they do make green gumdrops. If they're brown, you can use chocolate-covered peanuts or even raisins.)

**5.** One red licorice whip.

**6.** Twenty or more cinnamon red-hot candies.

**7.** One white birthday candle.

# How to Make It

**1.** Have a grown-up bake the cake.
(If they're nice, maybe they'll let you help.)

**2.** When the cake is cool, spread the face frosting over the top and sides.

**3.** Spread the other frosting along the top and down the sides to look like the chicken pox person's hair. Be careful. It's hard to fix mistakes.

**4.** Plop the two gumdrops where the eyes go.

**5.** Add an extra dab of face frosting for the nose.

**6.** Break off a mouth-size piece of the licorice whip and lay it this way where the mouth goes.
Eat the rest.

**7.** Gently press the red-hot candies all over the face. The more, the better.

**8.** Stick one birthday candle near the side of the mouth so it looks like a thermometer.

**9.** Have a grown-up light the candle.

**10.** Sing your version of "Happy Chicken Pox to You."

**11.** Hope you don't get chicken pox, too.